Seven Simple and Slightly Silly Stories

John Foley

Drawings by Grant Cathro

QuizzicalWorks

Coming next!

Another Seven Simple and Slightly Silly Stories

including '**The Last Raindrop**', '**Donner and Blitzen**', '**The Lost Key**', '**The Wasp in the Olive Tree**', and '**The Snooty Puddle**':

One day, not so long ago and just for a very short time, there was a puddle in the middle of the road. Rain had been falling for several hours and the road – more a lane really – was in a bad state with scattered potholes and cracks almost from one end to the other. To the left of the puddle in question – let's call it George for the sake of argument – and to the right of it there were other puddles. Most of them were larger and one or two much larger, but to George slap bang in the middle they were of no consequence, because although George was quite small it was deeper. It also had in it flecks of gold...

For Macmillan Cancer Support
and The Silver Line

Contents

Cat and Mouse 9

The Battle in the Washtub 21

The Ants Who Wanted to Cross the Road 33

The Tooth Fairy 45

The Cockroach and the Condemned Man 57

The Mayfly 69

An Unwelcome Visitor 79

Cat and Mouse

The cat crouched on one side of the hole, the mouse on the other. They had been that way for some time and they were both beginning to get rather bored.

For more than three months the summer house in the country had been filled with luggage and laughter and busy comings and goings. Now the summer was over. Early that morning everyone had departed; the house was closed and empty. Only the cat was left behind.

'You still there?' said the mouse.

'I'm still here,' replied the cat, staring hard at the hole.

'What are you waiting for?'

'For you to come out.'

'And then what?'

'Then I shall catch you and eat you.'

'Why?'

'Why?' said the cat. He had not expected all these questions and was quite taken aback.

'Yes, why? Are you so hungry?'

What impertinence! thought the cat. 'That's none of your business,' he said haughtily. 'But if you must know, it's my duty.'

'Duty?' said the mouse. 'To whom?'

'To those who keep and feed me, of course; who stroke and scratch my back.'

'And call you silly names and pull your tail?'

The cat was silent.

'And where are they now?' said the mouse. 'They've gone, haven't they? Forgotten you, left you behind without even a saucer of milk. What about their duty to you?'

'They'll be back as soon as they remember.'

'You think so?'

'Oh yes, I'm sure of it,' the cat replied hastily. Until that moment, the idea of being forgotten had not occurred to him.

'Poor thing,' said the mouse. 'Fancy being abandoned.'

The cat tried a little purr to show he wasn't worried, but it didn't work. The seed of doubt had been sown. 'Abandoned.' He didn't recognise the word, but it had an even more unpleasant ring to it than 'forgotten'. Surely it was a mistake. They were forgetful like that sometimes: didn't let him back in at night, didn't leave enough food when they were out all day long. But 'abandoned'? No, it was not possible; and if it was, why? What had he done to deserve it? Hurriedly he searched his conscience. The lamp he had knocked over? The piece of salmon he'd taken from the dining-room table?

'I thought they'd left it there for me,' he said out loud.

'What?' said the mouse.

'Nothing,' the cat answered gloomily. 'Just talking to myself.' He took a deep breath and dug his claws in the carpet, then remembered himself and quickly withdrew them. The night before last there had been angry talk of fleas and a special collar (he didn't like the sound of that, whatever it was). But that was one of the hazards of a hot, dry summer; and anyway – he thought, giving himself an absentminded scratch – what's a few fleas among friends? No, as far as he was concerned, his conscience was clear. Well, almost. There was of course that puddle on the bedroom floor, but it was such a little one! Besides, what was he supposed to do behind a closed door for hours and hours?

'Cat?'

'What is it?'

'You hungry yet?'

The cat thought quickly and came to the conclusion that he was. He'd quite forgotten the time. Already the long shadows of evening were creeping across the carpet. Somewhat stiff and cross-eyed from so much staring, he got up and stretched, and then at last – trying not to sound too interested – he answered: 'Perhaps I could manage a little something.'

'Splendid!' said the mouse. 'Because I've been thinking. You're out there, I'm in here. That does seem rather pointless. Now I'm a kind-hearted, generous sort of chap – not like some I could name, as you well know!'

The cat didn't know anything of the sort. He was young, he lived a quiet, sheltered life, and was not on familiar terms with this mouse or any other. Nevertheless, not wishing to appear ignorant, he agreed.

'I can't complain about my life,' the mouse continued. 'It's been long and happy. But now I'm tired. No, worse than tired, I'm bored. My wife is dead, the children have all left home, and if your lot are coming back for you–'

'Oh yes, of course!'

'Then it will be very quiet. After summer comes winter always, and that's no fun, I can assure you, when the house is empty and the cupboard bare. Just between ourselves there is this old dear who comes in now and again to clean and dust, but she's so unbearably tidy there's never a crumb. I tell you, one more winter like the last will be the death of me! So, here's what I propose: I come out, we have a chase, and then you catch me. Mind you, I'll give you a good run just to make it more exciting. You look as though you could do with the exercise – if you don't mind my saying so,' the mouse added, for he was very polite.

Under any other circumstances the cat would have minded very much, for he was plump, if not shamefully overweight for his size – always eating between meals whatever he could scrounge or steal, even the stale bread left out for the birds. Just at that moment, however, he was a little too confused to take offence. 'Do I understand correctly?' he asked. 'You actually want me to chase you?'

'Yes.'

'And catch you?'

'Yes, again.'

'And eat you?'

'Thrice right, my feline friend!' the mouse cried gleefully. 'You will go far.'

There was a lull in the conversation while the cat considered this strange proposal. He gave himself an embarrassed lick behind the ears and straightened his whiskers and did all those other important things that cats do when they don't quite know what to say.

'You don't sound very enthusiastic,' said the mouse. 'You have caught us before, haven't you?'

The cat hung his head. He was feeling very stupid.

'Oh, good gracious goodness,' said the mouse. 'Just my luck, a beginner. Well, can't be helped, I suppose. But do try not to make a hash of it. One clean break just below my skull. That's all I ask. None of this dabbing me around the floor and tossing me up in the air. It does rather prolong the matter.'

'But isn't that expected?' asked the cat.

'For tenderising? Making us more chewable? Stuff and nonsense!' the mouse snorted. 'And anyway, is it fair? I mean to say would you like it? I remember my poor wife went through agony with an ugly cat from the farm down the road.'

The cat had a vague feeling that that 'stuff and nonsense' was all part and parcel of a timeless ritual, but rather than be thought even more of a fool he asked instead, 'Will it hurt much?'

'Don't you worry your head about things like that. You just do it properly and make sure you enjoy me, tail and all.'

'Tail?' said the cat.

'Oh yes, the tail is a must, quite a delicacy. And yet so many of your lot leave it behind. My dear wife had such a beautiful one and that stupid farm cat didn't even look twice at it.'

This cat didn't think he'd look twice at it either. He was beginning to wish he had never started this. He had quite lost his appetite and at that moment would have liked nothing better than a long drink of cool, fresh milk. But there wasn't any. 'That's very... er, very...' he mumbled, searching for the right word.

'Sporting?' the mouse suggested. 'Yes, it is rather, but then you'll be doing me a favour. Oh, you can't imagine how dull my life is when there's no one here! You're sure they'll come back for you?'

'Any moment now,' insisted the cat, though not quite as confidently as before.

The mouse hesitated. What did he really want? A final fling, one last glorious game? Or the damp chill of winter, rheumatism, that awful silence? Forgotten. Abandoned. He shuddered. 'Well,' he said briskly, 'let's get on with it before I change my mind. Close your eyes, count to a hundred, and then come after me.'

'A hundred?' said the cat. 'That's too many.'

'Fifty then.'

'Still too many. You see,' he confessed, 'I've really no head for figures.' And he hadn't; he could count up to twenty-seven, but that was only by missing out a few numbers here and there. 'Why don't you just shout when you're ready.'

'Oh, very well,' said the mouse. 'But don't forget: a chase to the death and no holds barred. Agreed?'

'Agreed.'

'Cross your heart and hope to die?'

'Yes, yes!' the cat said irritably. He shut his eyes tightly.

The mouse peeped out of the hole, and then scrabbled across the carpet, out of the living-room and into the kitchen.

'Come and find me!' he called at last.

The cat opened his eyes. He hadn't the faintest idea where to start, and really didn't want to; but he had given his word. He had a quick stretch and scratch, and then after a brief look under the sofa, behind the desk, and a few other places where he hoped the mouse wouldn't be, he ran into the hall. Still no mouse.

'No, no,' came the voice. 'You're getting cold.'

'Of course, the kitchen,' muttered the cat. He dashed in there.

'Too late, too late!' urged the mouse, already halfway up the stairs. 'You'll have to do better than that.'

And that was how it was. Up and down the stairs, back and forth through empty cupboards and wardrobes, in every nook and cranny from the cellar to the attic, round and round and round they went.

Darkness fell outside, and inside too. But the cat could still see. So could the mouse, and he couldn't remember when he'd enjoyed himself so much. He felt young again; he was having a wonderful time!

The cat, on the other hand, was not. For him it was beyond a game. He wanted to catch the mouse, to get it over with. He was now doing his very best, but it just wasn't good enough. Every time he got to where the mouse was, he wasn't anymore.

'Coo-ee!' came the voice. 'Over here.' And a moment later, 'No, stupid, over this way now!'

'Not so fast,' groaned the cat. He felt sick and dizzy, he had a pain in his chest, and his head was pounding. 'Please, just a little rest.'

'A promise is a promise,' said the teasing voice so close. 'To the death!'

And off they went again. Suddenly the cat could take no more. His heart burst through his throat and with a rasping groan he sank heavily to the ground.

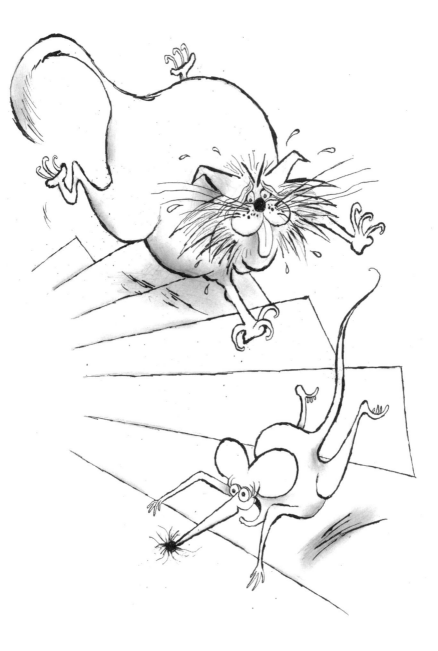

If it's true that cats have nine lives no one had bothered to tell him about it. He lay still and silent. At first the mouse thought it was just a trick, but the minutes on the old grandfather clock in the hall ticked by and still the cat didn't stir. The mouse crept out of his hiding place.

'Come on, cat. You can do it. You almost caught me that time.'

No response. The mouse crept closer.

'Don't give up now. My tail is itching.'

Still no response.

'You promised,' the mouse pleaded, face to face. He tweaked the cat's whiskers, kicked him, nipped him, pulled his tail, did absolutely everything he could think of to annoy the cat and get him moving again. But it was no use; there was not a flicker of life.

'Oh dear, oh dear,' said the mouse at last. 'I don't know what the world is coming to. Can't rely on anyone these days.' And with a deep mournful sigh he shambled back to his lonely hole, unhappily dragging the uneaten tail behind him.

The Battle in the Washtub

No one knew where the sock came from or how it came to be included with the rest of the laundry. It just appeared. One moment all the clothes were blinded with soapsuds and thoroughly agitated with hot water coursing through every fibre, the next moment the first rinse began – and there it was, tangled but undeniably different. The dress shirt was the first to notice.

'What the devil!' he cried, disengaging an arm. 'Who are you?'

'I beg your pardon, sir,' said the sock respectfully, for though somewhat dazed and surprised to find himself where he was he quickly identified the speaker as a cut above the others. 'Allow me to introduce myself–'

'Why, hello there,' said a T-shirt, plain and dull-witted but a terrible gossip nonetheless. 'Not seen your like before. What are you?'

'Well, actually,' began the sock, trying to stretch his full knee-length to show off a tasteful geometric pattern in red, grey and black.

'He's an argyle, stupid,' said an old blue stocking

who knew about these things.

'Yes, indeed. That I am.'

'Oh', replied the T-shirt, and none the wiser swirled away to be first to tell the others.

A bit of a flirt on the sly the stocking edged closer. 'I do hope we'll be fast friends. Meantime, welcome to the family.' And before the argyle could answer she too had swirled away.

'Welcome be hanged!' the dress shirt snorted. To be thrown in the wash with such an assortment of everyday riffraff was bad enough, but to have to share with unannounced outsiders – especially one so handsome – was intolerable. 'Who let you in?'

'Ah! there you have me, I'm afraid,' said the argyle, still intertwined with the shirt. 'To be quite candid I haven't the foggiest notion. The last thing I remember–'

'Saints preserve us!' complained a passing glove who only the week before had attended a very smart wedding and was now filled with pious zeal. 'It's not right. Far too much intimacy among the lower orders as it is without being invaded by multi-coloured impostors.'

'Exactly!' agreed the dress shirt, trying to disentangle the other arm. 'I don't approve of all this mixing. Time was when inferior garments and man-made coloureds would have been washed separately.'

'I couldn't agree more!' said the glove. 'All this equality is so demoralising.'

'Equality! Balderdash!' the shirt cried. 'I'm white!'

'Not with that wine stain you're not!' scoffed a grey shirt who had seen better days.

'This is outrageous,' wailed the white shirt. 'I deserve respect!'

'Respect? In 'ere? You'll be lucky!' said the left half of a rather ragged pair of gardening socks.

'Yeah, don't be so stuffy,' said the right half.

'All very well for you to talk,' the glove shrieked. 'You have nothing left to lose.'

'What did you say?' growled the gardening socks together.

'Nothing left to lose!' the glove repeated scornfully.

'I say,' said the argyle, 'please don't fight.'

'Mind your own business,' said the shirt. 'At least we know where we come from.'

'Probably some cheap foreign muck,' said a third shirt coming up behind.

'Now there I have to draw the line,' the argyle insisted. 'I have the finest pedigree. I'm an Argyle with a capital A, pure lambswool through and through and not cheap in the slightest. Why even Harrods would be proud–'

'Hark at his lordship!' screamed a rather vulgar nylon sock. 'Harrods, no less. Pass the caviar, dear!'

Meanwhile the gossip, with a little help from the flirt, had spread the word and now everyone crowded round as best they could to catch a glimpse, a touch even of the strange sock. There was a lot of pushing and shoving and the argyle thought them the oddest collection he'd ever been in with. Clearly someone somewhere had made a mistake and he hoped he would soon be retrieved. Until then, however, he'd make the best of it and force himself to enjoy being the centre of attention.

'No, seriously,' he continued, 'kings have worn my ancestors as they tramped through the heather shooting grouse—'

Another shirt, a cotton polyester mixture with rather dubious socialist leanings, took immediate exception to this statement. 'We'll have none of that high and mighty superior monarchistic claptrap in here—'

'Let him be,' said a bedsock sleepily. 'I think it's rather romantic.'

'You would.'

'And why not?' said the bedsock's companion. 'When you lie around as much as we do a little bit of intrigue doesn't come amiss.'

'Yes!' agreed the left gardening sock. 'I for one am sick and tired of seeing the same boring old faces week in week out—'

'How dare you!' said the dress shirt indignantly. 'You don't see me every week.'

'Good thing, too.'

'I shouldn't be here at all.'

'So you keep saying,' said the T-shirt.

'But I shouldn't, dammit!'

'Clearly nor should I,' said the argyle and, unaware of the row he was causing, foolishly continued his boasts. 'You know, I've led a pretty adventurous and, I may add, distinguished life. Of course, in my position–'

'If you're so special,' the glove interrupted, 'where's the rest of you?'

'Rest of me?'

'Your other half.'

'Better half, no doubt,' sneered someone else.

'My goodness, old chap,' said the argyle, 'you've put your finger on it there. Where, indeed?'

A silence followed as they all tumbled round a few times, thinking deeply. Finally, as that rinsing water drained away the argyle spoke again. 'I have to admit I'm stumped. There must be another half, unless of course, ha ha!' (and here he laughed, for even in this predicament he was not without a sense of humour), 'my owner is a uniped.'

'Eh?' said the right gardening sock and the T-shirt together.

'He means one-legged,' the blue stocking explained.

'Tramping through the heather?' sneered the polyester shirt. 'Oh yes, very likely.'

'Happens to the best of us, old chap.'

'Must be awfully lonely,' said one bedsock clinging to the other.

'If it is, I've never noticed. But then I can't quite remember. Perhaps I've got amnesia–'

Again the blue stocking explained to the ignorant: 'Loss of memory.'

'Then why didn't he say so?' cried the shirt. 'All these fancy words. Pretentious toe-rag!'

'Can I help it if I'm educated?' said the argyle. 'Have to be in my position. Obviously you've never considered the honourable responsibility we socks have to adorn the feet and keep them warm.'

'Responsibility, yes! You're so right,' the bedsocks agreed. 'Nothing worse than cold feet, stuck out there at the end of the body all neglected.'

'Best place for them,' muttered the polyester.

'We heard that!' cried the bedsocks.

'You were meant to.'

'Come now, sneer and cavil if you must,' said the argyle. 'But when all's said and done we are the unsung heroes.'

'Heroes? How the blazes do you work that out?' the dress shirt demanded jealously.

'Think about it, old chap. The head, shoulders, chest, and all the other bits may be above us, but what do they rest on? The feet, of course. And who moves the whole lot from place to place? Again, the feet. Truly we cover the most important part of a body–'

This statement provoked an outcry from several garments. The argyle ignored them and continued:

'—the root of all feeling, the extremities of the heart and soul—'

'Pompous nonsense!' cried the polyester.

'I object to all that,' said the glove. 'It's the hands that count most.'

'I hardly think so or they'd be better protected,' said the argyle. 'No, no, my dear, it's the feet, and we their noble servants are all too often taken for granted. You, alas, are merely an accessory.'

'Accessory!' screamed the glove, and cruelly insulted broke into loud sobs.

'I've never heard such insolence in all my life,' said the dress shirt, putting his arm around the glove to comfort her.

'Elitist!' cried the polyester.

Another rinse came and went.

The argyle ignored them all. He knew now they were a vulgar lot as well as plain, stupid and ugly, but he was not one to waste a captive audience. Indeed, the thought suddenly occurred to him that it was his duty, his destiny even, to educate and enlighten them. On and on he pontificated about the history of socks, social, political, economic; the geography of socks and their owners' habitat; even the science of sock manufacture – and all this to the delight and amazement of the other socks who had never realised they occupied such an important place in the progress of mankind.

'Let us not forget, too, the language of hosiery,' he said grandly.

'Oooh, you're right there!' said one bedsock. '"A sock in the jaw"'

'"Put a sock in it"!' said the other.

'And then of course, "Sock it to me",' the old blue stocking suggested, for though learned and rather prim and proper she liked to keep in touch with the vernacular of modern living. Such knowledge often came in handy with flirting.

'Good grief!' thought the argyle. 'What philistines!' Dutifully he moved quickly from the general merits of being a sock to the more elevated specifics of being an argyle.

Finally, the dress shirt could stand it no longer. He had always loved to regale the rest of the laundry with stories of the parties and receptions he attended (most of which had never happened), and now suddenly in this motley gathering what should have been his eminence and respectability were counting for nothing. And to cap it all he was still caught up with this confounded upstart! The very buttons on him burned red with rage. Savagely he yanked his arm and felt a splitting pain in the shoulder. The argyle, still engrossed in his own words, noticed nothing, not even when the shirt, now intent on murder, drew back his arms and swung with all his might. But, thrown off balance as the final rinse began, both arms missed the argyle and instead hit the polyester and the poor

glove who howled in agony. The glove's companion came to the rescue and by mistake in the confusion of being hurled apart and together throttled a bedsock who kicked the T-shirt who smothered a handkerchief who attacked the polyester – and the battle was on. Oblivious to the mayhem the dress shirt swung again and this time found his target and strangled and wrenched and battered and cuffed with all his belligerent might until the foolish argyle screamed and shrieked his last.

Never had a washtub seen such massacre before. Everyone took sides that day and then took sides again till at the end no one quite knew who was for whom or why. Except the dress shirt. As the final spin was spun and the last wring wrung and all the clothes settled in a damp, exhausted heap he alone was jubilant. Of the argyle, so proud and special, there remained not a shred of poise or dignity; nothing in fact but a sodden mass of woolly fluff to clog the drainage.

But victory often comes at a price, and for the dress shirt life was never the same again. With lost buttons and a torn arm, not to mention a mangled collar and cuff too he was not considered worth the mending. The next day he was tossed into a clothes' recycling bin where he met some even worse characters. But that's quite another story.

The Ants Who Wanted to Cross the Road

A family of ants wanted to cross the road. It was not a large family as ant-families go, and the road was not exactly a motorway, but it was certainly bigger and busier than the peaceful country lane that had been their only experience of human highways – until now. Early one morning and quite unexpectedly men had come with roaring bulldozers and gravel trucks and huge pots stinking of tar. They were enlarging the lane, widening and extending it all the way to the busy road that now stretched for miles to the left and to the right of the ant-family. Called 'progress', this was guaranteed to make life quicker and more convenient for the traffic rushing impatiently down to the coast and then across the new bridge to the land beyond.

The ants, unfortunately, did not understand this. But why should they? For while it made life easier for the humans, cars, lorries, buses, and whatever else thundered by, it made life most inconvenient for the ants. In the course of all this noisy, bustling 'progress' their anthill had been destroyed, quite flattened. The happy, thriving home that had been there for longer than any of them could remember was no more. Some had escaped; those who had not now lay buried beneath the new tarmac.

A garrulous wasp told one of the survivors of a marvellous anthill not so far away. There, he was sure, they would all be most welcome. This assumption, by the way, was hotly disputed: ants are not renowned for mixing too well. However, the choice was tempting. So, taking their lives in their legs, they set off.

But what seems not so far away as the wasp flies can be a marathon to an ant. Several days and several nights they had been travelling, and even with as little luggage as they carried on their backs the journey seemed endless. It was summer, it was hot, and at last as they stood on the verge of the wide road they were tired, disgruntled, and not a little suspicious.

'You can't trust wasps,' said one, rubbing his feet.

'Never could, never should. Ruffians and scavengers, the lot of them!' said another, the critic in the family (but as he was also very young no one ever took much notice).

'All sounds like pie in the sky to me,' complained a third. 'How do we know what lies beyond?'

'That's life,' said the first who had now finished rubbing his feet and so felt a little more philosophical.

'We go on!' said a fourth sternly. He was quite a senior ant and therefore considered he had the right to make these momentous decisions.

But there was the problem. The whole point of the

mission was to reach the marvellous anthill, and to do that they had to go on. But how? The road before them was busy day and night.

A party of scouts was quickly dispatched. All morning they scurried up and down the grass verge looking for a safe way across, but there was none.

'Let's just go!' said the senior ant. 'Some of us are bound to make it to the other side.'

'What a comforting thought,' said the critic, 'but perhaps I don't feel quite so lucky as you.'

'If I may be allowed to offer my knowledge on these subjects,' said a rather scholarly ant, 'I suggest that we wait.'

'Wait?' growled the senior ant.

'Oh yes. It's really quite simple. You see that signpost over there? Well, I've just read it!' said the ant proudly. He really was a clever ant, and he really could read – and that's not quite as ridiculous as it sounds. His grandmother had had the good fortune to be born into a family that lived right under the town library, and it was with her that he had studied this very special subject. Because of reading he knew a lot of things. In fact, he was so bright that he could have taken exams (and might even have passed them too), but he had little use for such trifles. It was enough for him to be clever and as he liked to call it – 'antelligent'. No, you're right, and none of the ants thought it a very good joke either, but he found it extremely amusing and as far as he was concerned that was what mattered. Now as to why he alone had learnt to read and his brothers and sisters hadn't (for, after all, weren't they just as related to the grandmother?) well, that's how it is sometimes, and anyway it's also quite another story.

'You and your reading!' sneered the critic, who despised cleverness of any kind.

'Yes, me and my reading. And if you could read you'd know that the sign states quite clearly that this road will be closed soon, and when that happens it will be perfectly safe to cross.'

'And when's that?'

'When they're ready to join our lane up to this one. A day or two. Perhaps even sooner.'

'Pooh!' said a particularly headstrong ant in disgust.

'Pooh!' said another (as matching twins they always thought alike). 'We want to get to wherever we're going right now!'

'Right now,' echoed the twin.

'Ohhh,' moaned a female ant. 'I don't think I shall ever get anywhere ever again. I'm lame for life, I'm sure of it.'

A male ant, who rather fancied his chances with the female, quickly offered to carry her across.

'You will not!' said a jealous cousin. 'You'll carry me before you carry her. I'm much more tired and much more deserving.'

'Pooh!' said the headstrong ant again. 'I'm not going to hang around listening to you lot bickering hour after hour. I, for one, am leaving now.'

'And I, for two!' added his twin. And so, leave they did. But scarcely had they begun their journey than a motor bike hurtled by, and that, sadly, was the end of them.

'That's what comes of being stupid,' remarked the clever ant.

Somewhat disheartened, the other ants decided that perhaps, after all, they should wait a while. So, they did. Unfortunately – ants being what they are – it was not long before their impatience got the better of them. New attempts were made upon the road, but each one ended in disaster. A car crushed seven, another motor bike three more. A heavy lorry flattened one so completely there wasn't even a damp patch left behind.

Night fell, the moon rose, the stars came out. Still the ants tried, and all the time the family grew smaller and smaller.

'Thought you said the road would soon be closed?' moaned one of his brothers.

'It will, it will,' the clever ant insisted. 'Trust me.'

The night wore on, the moon went down, and slowly day began to lighten the sky, the trees, the grass verge and the road until...

'Listen!' cried one of the ants.

They listened. 'I can't hear anything,' said the senior ant at last.

'Exactly!' the first ant said. 'The road must be closed. Let's go!'

The clever ant was not convinced. 'No, wait! Be patient just a while longer, until we're quite sure.'

'You be patient if you like but we're going now!'

Just then a hedgehog plodded by, and one of the cousins had the bright idea: why not hitch a lift?

'Oh yes, and save my aching legs,' said the female ant.

'Too old,' said the critic.

'I beg your pardon?' said the female indignantly.

'That thing is too old. He'll never make it.'

'Nonsense,' said the senior ant. 'He's in his prime, like me! Why, a fitter, healthier specimen I've not crawled over for many a moon. Come on, all aboard!'

'Well, I'm staying,' the clever ant said.

'Too old,' complained the critic again. Even so, he didn't want to be left behind with the ant who could read so he, too, joined the others.

For once, however, the critic was right. The poor hedgehog was long past his prime and, like the straw that broke the camel's back, the weight of so many passengers (for there were still quite a few) proved too much, and halfway across the road his heart gave way.

'Ooooh, do you think he's dead?' asked the ant who had suggested hitching a lift.

'Of course he's dead, you ignorant clot!' cried the critic.

'Oh, what shall we do?' wailed the stranded passengers.

'Didn't I tell you he was too old?' the critic continued. 'Sometimes you haven't the sense you were born with; if you were born with any, which I doubt!'

The ant to whom these unkind words were addressed naturally took umbrage. He attacked the critic.

'No time for that now,' urged the senior ant. 'Everyone off! Make a dash for cover!'

The two ants ignored him. Others joined in, and in no time they were all at it, nipping and pinching in their ant-like way as if there was no tomorrow – which for them, unfortunately, there wasn't. So busy were they with their squabbling and blaming each other for being too fat or too heavy or too stupid that they never saw the juggernaut. No, that's not quite true; one of them did but his cries went unheard. All too soon the monster was upon them. It crushed the dead hedgehog, and of course all the ants with it.

Now only the clever ant remained on the grass verge. He sensed the tragedy through his antennae but felt neither pity nor interest.

'Can't say I didn't warn them,' he sighed, and quickly thought about something else.

Left on his own the clever ant began to feel rather bored and lonely, but he felt – no, he knew – he had right on his side, and that's always a boost to one's confidence.

He waited. And waited. And then, at last, and yet much sooner than he had expected, he sensed that the road really was closed and empty. The great moment had arrived. Carefully he looked right, then left, then right again, until he was quite satisfied.

'Well, here goes!' he said finally. And so he went, cautiously to begin with and then with a bit of a swagger. 'I may not be the fastest but I'll still be there before the others. Ha! That's a good one,' he chuckled. 'You see, it wasn't such a long wait,' he cried as he passed the flattened hedgehog.

When he came to the white line that ran down the centre of the road he paused to catch his breath. Behind him lay the old world; ahead the new. Proudly he surveyed the scene.

'There!' he exclaimed. 'I am the only one to come this far. I can read, and what's more I can understand what I read, and that is so important in these illiterate times. Why, I should be ruler of my own anthill. Yes, that's it: King Me! For surely that is what I deserve and nothing less will do. And all of it have I achieved because of my superior "antellect".' And there he stood in the middle of the road, puffing out his chest and feeling very smart and triumphant as the sun rose higher and higher in the blue summer sky.

At that moment a rather frustrated crow alighted on the tarmac beside him. Normally the crow wouldn't have looked twice at such a paltry insect, but he had overslept, and breakfast had been meagre.

'Huh,' he said grumpily. 'Not much of a mouthful, but better than nothing, I suppose.' And before the ant could protest, down came the beak and gobbled him up: the only one not to be squashed because he was so clever – which just goes to prove that it's no good standing around boasting of success when you're only halfway there.

The Tooth Fairy

The tooth fairy was in a dreadful tizzy. Someone somewhere had lost a tooth and, as everyone knows, when that happens it is the tooth fairy's duty to find it and replace it with a shiny new coin. This is a time-honoured custom in many lands and a well-respected job for any fairy who rises to the rank. Now it stands to reason that in order to fulfil such important work a tooth fairy must first know where and who the someone is. Alas, however, on this occasion that was the problem. The someone was not to be found, and so of course neither was the tooth.

All through the night the tooth fairy searched in vain, visiting this bedroom and that, each time carefully lifting a pillow for the lost tooth. But it was nowhere. That is not such a disgrace if it happens only once, but for this particular fairy it was the third time in a row. She knew only too well how close she was to losing her status altogether.

Fairies are everywhere, much more than we think. They're a strange lot; they have their little quirks and idiosyncrasies just as we do. Perhaps even more so. But unlike us they prefer to keep themselves to themselves as much as possible, which is why so little is known about them. For example, it would be utter chaos if they were free to waft around waving their wands whenever they felt like it (even if they had wands, which most of them don't). So, to keep them out of mischief they all have certain duties to perform, from the top down – for within the fairy world there exists a very definite order. There is a king, of course; a queen, too; and under them a great many lords and ladies. And then further down the ladder of power, yet not too far, come the tooth fairies, each one assigned to a measured district of human lands.

This particular fairy had always wanted such a job, but she was just one of many and there was a long waiting list. So, patiently, she waited. At last the day came. There was a vacancy for a new tooth fairy and as she was next in line and of good character she was called before the king and offered a short trial period.

To begin with, all went well and she delighted in her new freedom.

A six-year-old boy with tousled fair hair, fast asleep with a grin on his face, was her first mission. Her second, a four-year-old girl with her thumb in her mouth and long silky black hair that covered the pillow, was equally successful. But then the next night something went wrong, and the night after that, too.

'You know the rules,' said the king severely, as she stood before him for the second time shamefaced and empty-handed. 'I'll allow you just one more chance. But remember, if you can't do the job properly there are plenty of others who can.'

One more chance. Failure or success. The tooth fairy shivered as she thought of a distant cousin who had once so disgraced himself with tomfoolery and a black cat that he was banished for a whole year to serve as guardian of a toy train set. For the first few days he quite enjoyed himself. Dutifully he polished the rails, mended the points, and kept the model station spotlessly clean. But no one ever came to play with the train and as the weeks dragged on he felt terribly alone and miserable. That was the worst of his punishment, for fairies need freedom and affection and success just as much as human beings. Of course, it wouldn't be quite that bad for her since she would not be banished. Nevertheless, a third failure would mean the end of her career. She would certainly be demoted, downgraded to a footling task like keeping an eye on someone's pet hamster or sitting in a doll's house to shoo the moths from the furniture. She shuddered at the thought of this last punishment as dolls' houses were becoming increasingly scarce and the few that remained were often to be found only in museums or worse: relegated to cold and dusty attics that no one visited, apart from the rats and... Oh, the thought was too awful!

'No!' she cried aloud as she travelled the starlit sky. She had to get it right. Surely the task couldn't be that difficult. As the night wore on, however, her hopes grew fainter and fainter. Soon it would be dawn and once again she would return empty-handed.

Suddenly, just as she was reconciling herself to her failure, she sensed what she was searching for. Yet was it? As she drew closer she sensed too that it was not a little boy or girl who had lost the tooth, neither was it under a pillow as it should be.

Then she saw him clearly: an old man in pyjamas and dressing gown.

Sitting at a table, he was examining his mouth with a small mirror and great concentration. Now and again he paused to rub his cheek and groan angrily and mutter in language that was really quite violent.

The tooth fairy hesitated. This was not at all what she expected.

She was not quite sure how to deal with such a situation. No one had really explained this sort of anger to her. The lamp on the table was bright and glaring, and a cold harsh light filled the room with huge unfriendly shadows. They made her feel rather afraid, though she didn't know why. But a tooth is a tooth, she thought boldly. She hadn't waited for the job all this time to lose it so soon. By hook or by crook she would do whatever had to be done. Thus, determined to secure the tooth she pushed her fear behind her and went in.

The man was not nearly as old as she supposed. He just looked that way. He had never been kind to anyone, and in return life had not been kind to him – or to his teeth. Over the years, at considerable expense and discomfort, they had all been drilled and filled and capped and crowned until there was scarcely anything left of the originals. Except for two. One of those now lay on the table in front of him.

The man had pulled out the tooth in a rage of pain. A piece of bloodstained string was still tied around it. The other end of the string, unattached, dangled over the edge of the table and shook every time the unhappy

man thumped the top. And he thumped it often. The tooth had taken a lot of wiggling and tugging till at last it was out. But still the pain continued.

'Dentists!' he snarled. 'All that money down the drain!' He struck the table again then clutched his jaw as a fresh spasm attacked him.

Silent and invisible, the fairy hovered by his side, watching him and wondering how to get the tooth. Although not exactly forbidden to show herself, it was nevertheless not encouraged.

'Only in exceptional cases,' the king advised when she accepted the job. 'We don't want to alarm people. It doesn't help them and only gives us a bad name. Remember your foolish cousin and the black cat. We'll never be welcome in that house again.'

Certainly, she thought, it would alarm the man to see his tooth floating through the air and out of the window. It might make him even angrier and then she really would be in disgrace like her cousin. She decided this had to be an exceptional case and made herself visible.

Slowly aware of her presence, the man looked up. He seemed neither surprised nor puzzled by what he saw but stared at her a moment with cold, dull eyes till she felt quite uncomfortable.

'How did you get in here?' he said at last.

'You summoned me.'

'Summoned you? What are you on about? I don't know you.'

'I am the tooth fairy,' she answered proudly, hoping this would explain everything. It didn't. The man frowned deeply, thinking hard. 'I've come for your tooth,' she said and made a move for it.

The man was too quick. He snatched up the tooth and held it away from her, tight in the palm of his hand. 'Ever tried pulling one out with a piece of string? Doesn't really work.' Again he struck the table and moaned. 'And after all that it's the wrong one!'

'Please,' she said. 'I need it. I'll be in such trouble otherwise. '

'Hardly my concern. New to this lark, are you?'

She held out a shiny coin. 'I'll give you this in exchange.'

'Ha! You won't buy much with that,' he said, hardly glancing at it. 'Besides, I don't believe in fairies.'

'Oh, but you must!'

'Must! You dare stand there and tell me–' He cracked his knuckles and stared at her sullenly. 'You don't exist. You're just a figment of my imagination.'

'No! If that were true you could not see me as you see me now. Only if you believe–'

'Childish nonsense! Oh yes, there was a time when I believed all that nursery foolishness. Longer ago than I want to remember.' He sighed unhappily, then thumped the table. 'But you never came when I needed you. I waited all night, my tooth under my pillow. I waited and you never came!'

'But that was not me, nor even a cousin of mine,' she said, almost sure that such was true. 'Whoever it was neglected their duty and will probably have lost their job for it. Just as I shall lose mine.'

'This is ridiculous! Here am I talking to a... a... well, whatever you are, you can leave the way you came. I'm going to bed.' He stood up, dropped the tooth in his dressing-gown pocket out of her reach and began to walk away. Suddenly he staggered against the wall, howling as the pain stabbed him again and again.

The fairy moved swiftly to his side and touched his cheek so lightly he wouldn't even have felt it. Touching humans was definitely forbidden but she could not bear to see him in such agony.

Through the darkness of the open window came a gentle breeze smelling of summer sunshine and freshly mown grass. With it there came the sound of cool spring water tinkling in a stone trough, of long-vanished faces, of laughter and life. It all reminded the man of a time so long ago, a time when he really did believe in fairies and was happy to do so.

'No, it's too late,' he said, struggling to expel the jumbled memories from his mind. 'It's all too late.'

'Don't say that,' the tooth fairy pleaded. 'It's never too late to believe. And you do even now, just a little. Or else I could not be here. If anyone loses a tooth and believes in us enough to put it under a pillow we have to come.'

'Aha!' he cried triumphantly. 'There I've got you. I never put it under my pillow!'

'But you could...' she suggested. 'Couldn't you?'

The man considered this for a moment, his face in a tight frown. Then all at once he cracked his fingers again, gave a snort, and began to laugh.

'Your toothache's gone,' she said.

'Perhaps. But of course it would. I pulled it out, didn't I?' Even so, he felt his cheek and carefully probed inside his mouth. The pain had gone completely; the swelling too. And that was so strange. The tooth he had pulled out was the wrong one. The tooth that was still in his mouth, the one that had been causing such pain should still be hurting, but it wasn't. He looked at the fairy. 'I don't understand,' he started to say.

Somewhere a clock struck five. An early morning bus rumbled down the street.

'Please,' said the fairy. 'There's not much time. I beg you, don't send me away without it. I shall be disgraced.'

Again there came a breeze of summer through the cold unfriendly room. In the depths of his heart something stirred. A warm soothing glow spread through his body. He hurried to the bedroom and put the tooth under the pillow. 'Go on, before I come to my senses and change my mind.'

The tooth fairy needed no prompting. Quickly she moved to the bed, found the tooth and in its place left the shiny coin. 'Thank you,' she said.

'You know,' he murmured, 'you look just as I

imagined you would. I mean, all those years ago when I....'

But already she was gone.

The man lifted the pillow: the coin was still there. He smiled and turned to the window. Far away in the east the sun began to rise. It was going to be a beautiful day.

The Cockroach and the Condemned Man

Old he was. Crippled he was. Unsociable he was not. For a cockroach, that is. And even now, though rather befuddled and still trapped in the condemned cell, he remembered his triumph as if it were yesterday.

So many of his family shunned the company of humans. They would scurry into hiding whenever one of these loud, two-legged beings came near. But not him. He was fascinated by them, and ever since his first – almost fatal – experience he had tried to understand their odd, quirky ways. One moment he was amused, the next indignant and exasperated by their unfair treatment, by the endless insults and attacks on him and his kind. They called him dirty, disgusting, loathsome; they said he spread disease. Be that as it may (though he didn't believe such ridiculous accusations), what was a poor chap supposed to do? Starve to death? Give up living altogether?

As just another insect trying to eke out a comfortable existence, were his habits any worse than all the other creatures who shared the same space? He certainly felt a lot cleaner in his ways than some of the humans he'd come across in the royal castle where he and his family lived.

And talking of families: he came from one that was 300 million years old. (This extraordinary fact he had quickly digested while nibbling through a thick volume of natural history in the castle library one damp, chilly afternoon.) Surely that should count for something. Such an ancient family tree should be respected, admired, not detested. Three hundred million years. Why, that was far older than any human beings, or even cats and dogs.

Cats. Dogs. Now there was a mystery he had long pondered. The place was full of them. They were everywhere, barking and sniffing and mewing and scratching. And to hear the way the humans billed and cooed over them – much more than they did over their own kind – made absolutely no sense. It obviously meant something, but what? Could it be the fact that they had four legs that was special? Did two extra legs make such a difference? No, it could not be that. After all, he himself had six: two more than either the dogs or the cats, and so logically he should be more popular. Yet he was loathed. Perhaps they were jealous of his sleek, shiny black body – of which he was exceedingly proud. No, it couldn't be that either, for there was one particular dog whose body was sleek and shiny and black, and it was prized more highly than all the others put together. His appetite then? Could it be that? No, for unlike them he did not have to be pampered once or even twice a day with food; indeed, he could go without eating a morsel for anything up to two months (if absolutely necessary).

His smell then? No, certainly not, for the dogs were unquestionably smellier. So it must be because of his size, being just too small to fondle or play with. But no one ever gave him a chance! The more he pondered this mystery the more it puzzled him and, being blessed with an enquiring mind, the more it puzzled him the more he determined to find an answer.

'Some of us are made to be loved, others to be loathed,' said his mother wisely. 'That's the way things are in this world and it's no good you prattling on about changing them, especially with that two-legged lot.'

'Well, it's not right, and it's just not fair!' he protested, and he made up his mind to prove her wrong. If what the book in the library told him was true (and though it was dry with a rather unpleasant aftertaste he saw no reason to disbelieve it) then in all those many, many years a cockroach must have befriended a human, and if it had been done before it could be done again. On the other hand, if it hadn't been done it was high time he put the matter right.

Over the next few months he travelled through the castle − farther than most of his kind cared or dared to go − in search of this friendship. And, of course, of good food and shelter − important considerations in the life of any self-respecting roach. The most obvious starting point was the huge bustling kitchen, but after a quick peek from the doorway he wisely decided not to enter. For one thing, it was far too hot and noisy; for another, he knew better than to risk the wrath of the large bellowing cook, who (it was rumoured)

frequently went on the rampage. Brandishing an old rolling pin, she would attempt to beat the living daylights out of mice, rats, the poor scullery maids, and any other verminous pests who crossed her path. The cockroach knew only too well to which category he belonged.

He tried the library where he'd discovered his ancestry. But that was too dry and musty, and humans rarely seemed to set foot in there long enough for him to make any sort of favourable impression. He tried the royal apartments: bedchambers, dressing rooms, closets and cupboards, not to mention endless draughty hallways. But in spite of one pleasant afternoon spent chewing on a very fine silk ballgown he found the experience rather dull and fruitless. He wandered briefly into the drawing room (too many dogs), the dining room (too much cigar smoke), even the billiard room, where the humans seemed to be concerned only with knocking coloured balls from one end of a table to the other. He journeyed to less regal parts of the castle; through the armoury and guard room, through the stables and soldiers' quarters, through this corridor and that. Always it was the same disappointing story: either he passed unnoticed, or his presence aroused such fury that he didn't dare stay around to explain.

Whenever he returned home to the damp comfort of the cupboard under the backstairs, his mother would ask the same question and he would shake his head sadly and admit that he had not found a friend. 'But I will!' he declared boldly. 'There must be someone somewhere who won't loathe me.'

'Climbing too high for the likes of us,' muttered his grandfather, a sour, wizened roach who bitterly resented the fact that he had not been born into a better class of creature. Nevertheless, he was content to sit tight where he was, for he intended to live to a ripe old age. 'And you don't do that by gallivanting and poking your nose where you shouldn't. Know your place, or you'll come to a sticky end.'

'Squashed!' jeered his numerous brothers and sisters. 'Squashed he'll be and serves him right, for he's no better than the rest of us.'

'See how you put us at sixes and sevens with your foolish nonsense,' growled the grandfather. 'Hobnobbing with humans. Pah! Pride before a fall, you mark my words. First you go up in the world, then you come down. Aye, lad, with a nasty bump.'

'He's right. Isn't it enough to be a royal cockroach?' urged his mother for, living in a royal castle and being a bit of a snob, this was how she regarded herself. 'Give it up and enjoy yourself for what you are.'

So, to keep the peace, he did give it up. But he couldn't enjoy himself or his family. Try as hard as he did, always in the back of his mind lay the nagging conviction that they were wrong about humans and friendship, and if anyone could prove it then he was just the one.

This conviction became an obsession. He couldn't sleep for thinking about it. He lost weight. Finally, he could stand it no longer, and without even saying goodbye he set off to continue his search.

The weather was miserable, a cold drizzle was falling and the castle lay shrouded in fog. It was not at all the sort of weather for travelling, but then he had no intention of setting foot outside, convinced as he was that what he sought would be found within the walls.

How his quest brought him to the cell of the condemned man he could not say. He certainly remembered leaving the cupboard, wandering along dark dismal corridors and down passages and stairs where he'd never ventured before, until at length and quite by accident he came into the dungeons. In one of them he received a vicious swipe that sent him reeling and he barely escaped with his life. After that everything was a bit blurred. He remembered stumbling, then falling a long, long way – at the same time wondering if this must be what his grandfather meant by going down in the world. And then nothing.

When he came to his senses he was lying in the palm of the condemned man's hand. (As to how he knew the man was condemned – well, there are certain things a cockroach knows by instinct, and this was one of them.) He tried to move. He couldn't. All the breath had been knocked out of him and two of his legs were broken. But he felt no fear.

The man was squatting on the floor, rocking slowly backwards and forwards. He seemed so different from all the other two-leggeds. He was thin and gaunt, his face pale, his sunken eyes bloodshot and filled with a dreadful despair. It was this despair more than anything else that confused and upset the roach. He wanted to say something to the man to cheer him up, but nothing came into his head, and anyway they didn't speak the same language. And yet, as he looked into the man's face he saw the beginnings of a smile. It was just a little smile but enough to make the roach's heart leap, for he knew suddenly he had found his friend.

The cell was small: four walls covered with cracked and stained whitewash, a bare stone floor, and even with as little furniture – only a rusting bedstead and a rickety chair – there was hardly room enough to swing a cat. (This was a phrase he'd picked up on his travels, and as much as he disliked cats he could not imagine why anyone would want to swing one.) Overhead, far out of reach, was the grill through which he had fallen, and above that, suspended from somewhere in the darkness beyond, a gas lamp that sputtered dimly. All in all, it was cold, smelly, and rather depressing, but the roach didn't care. He had succeeded. He was loved not loathed.

The days went by. Nothing happened; nothing disturbed their peace. The man himself was almost cheerful. He would pace the cell, sit on the bed or squat on the floor, sometimes rocking silently, sometimes crooning, but always he held the cockroach gently in his hand, and with every passing hour seemed to love him more and more.

'If only they could see me now,' said the cockroach proudly, and he remembered the dog with the sleek, shiny black body who was prized more highly than all the others put together. 'Now I'm every bit as good as him, if not better!'

Just how long they spent together he could not tell. Hidden in the castle's depths with only the gas lamp which never went out, there was no difference between day and night. Every so often the grill would open, the slop bucket would be drawn up, emptied, and then come down again, and with it a small basket of food and water. It was their only link with the world beyond, and that's just how they liked it.

One day the bucket was drawn up as usual, but it did not come down again, and neither did the food. The cockroach knew then that something was going to happen.

The condemned man knew it too. He shuddered and began rocking violently back and forth. Then all at once he groaned and sat completely still, staring at the blank wall; and once again his eyes were filled with that dreadful despair. A large tear rolled down his cheek, hung for a moment in his beard then splashed onto the roach. The tear was wet and warm and salty.

There was a sharp noise above. A key turned in the lock, two heavy bolts were shot, the whole grill opened and an iron ladder was let down. Suddenly the roach understood. 'Let me come with you. Take me, too. I'm not afraid,' he cried soundlessly, but for the first time in his life he was terribly afraid. He tried to scurry up his friend's arm. The man shook his head and picked him off his tattered sleeve. He raised the roach to his lips, kissed him and gently dropped him under the bed, safely out of sight.

Now there were other men in the cell. They seized

the condemned man, dragged him to his feet and up the ladder. He made no protest; he did not look back.

Some time later the cockroach shivered, his antennae twitched. Were they playing tricks? Or did he really sense a drumroll in the distance and a crack as though something had snapped in two? Then the lamp sputtered and went out. He knew it would not be relit. It was all over and he was in empty darkness. But now he was afraid no longer. Instead there was a strange mixture of feeling sad and happy all at the same time. Happy because he had proved them wrong: he had befriended a human; and sad because the man was gone. But the saddest thing of all was that he could not get home, and so no one would ever know.

The Mayfly

The day was hot, the sun already high when the mayflies hatched in the pond. As soon as they were free of their egg cases they swam up through the water that had enveloped them for so long, rested briefly on the surface to dry their lacy wings and then flew away, eager for adventure.

That is, all but one mayfly who lagged behind in a cautious sort of way. He had a feeling about this bright new world, a strange feeling and not a very pleasant one. He could not say why or how, but he had it quite definitely and that was enough for him. He glanced down at his own reflection in the clear water and gasped: he looked so dainty and fragile.

'Wheee! Isn't this exciting?' cried a voice close by. Just in time he looked up to see one of his brothers skipping gaily over the surface. The next moment the brother was gone, dragged under and swallowed by a fish.

'Ho there, tiny!' roared a dragonfly hovering above. 'Another wonderful day!'

'No, it's not!' gasped the mayfly. 'Didn't you see?

My brother – just gobbled up.'

'Ha! Think no more about it. It's nothing.'

'Nothing? That can't possibly be so.'

'Sure can. Happens all the time.'

The mayfly did not want to hear such things. 'Of course, it was his own fault,' he stammered, 'being so irresponsible, prancing around, not looking–'

'You betcha! But that's life.'

'Life? But what if we all did that, where would we be?'

'Down a fish's gullet!' replied the dragonfly cheerfully. And in a brightly coloured flash he was off.

The mayfly was astounded: his worst suspicions were confirmed. 'Oh, this is no place for me!' he cried, and without looking left or right he flew up into the air then straight down again to a clump of weed by the edge of the pond. A large flower grew there and into it he dived headlong. He hadn't the faintest idea what kind of flower it was or even that it was beautiful and sweet-smelling. All he cared for now was safety and shelter.

'That was dreadful,' he panted, his heart beating wildly. 'This is a terrible world. I should never have been born!' And so saying, he wept and moaned.

He had not been there long, deep in miserable thought about how frightening and unfair life was, when there was a loud buzzing and suddenly a fat bee all striped in yellow and black with legs heavy-laden with pollen poked his head inside.

'Go away, go away!' screamed the mayfly. 'This is my flower!'

The bee was so startled he flew off again without even a protest.

'My flower?' thought the mayfly. 'Why yes, that's it. I'll just stay here where no one can touch me. I don't need to do anything but be, and surely I can do that just as easily here as anywhere else, and a lot more safely. Yes, clearly that's the answer. Thank goodness I was born so clever.' And for the first time in his life he brightened up, proud of his decision. He began to take a careful note of his surroundings. There was not much room deep inside the flower and it was rather dark but, he decided, compared to the horrors of the outside world it was warm and cosy and really quite acceptable. 'Yes, indeed! This should do me very nicely for the time being.'

And the beautiful, sweet-smelling flower did him very nicely, except for the odd disturbances outside and one or two intrusions. First there was the lady mayfly. 'This is the life!' she trilled happily, popping in to rest awhile. 'The world is so lovely. All the colours, the fragrant summer smells, such a wealth I never dreamed of. Won't you come and share with me?'

For a moment he was interested – well, that's only natural even among mayflies, and after all she was very attractive. But then he remembered himself and his determination to survive.

'Generous of you, but I think I'd rather not.'

'It's such fun!'

'I'm sure it is. But one does not survive on fun alone,' he replied pompously. 'Fun can be dangerous.'

'Oh,' said the lady, somewhat at a loss for words. 'Well then, I'll be seeing you.'

'I doubt it,' he muttered as she flew away. 'I'm glad I'm not so frivolous. Let her go flirting with fun and adventure and see how long she lasts. I know the dangers!' And as if to prove his point he peeked outside.

Before him stretched the pond, wide and shimmering in the sun. Glittering fish darted back and forth. An ugly frog sat noisily on a lily pad. A weasel with snarling lips and sharp teeth crept to the edge of the pond to drink. Warily he watched the weasel who watched the frog who watched a tall gangly bird wading in the shallows. Fascinated the mayfly watched all three. Suddenly the bird plucked a fish and swallowed it whole in two gulps. On the bank another bird ripped a worm from the soil and left it dangling and wriggling in its beak.

'Ugh, that's horrible! Disgusting!' cried the mayfly. If he had stayed to watch he might have seen even worse things, but he didn't. 'Thank goodness I'm safe here,' he said, and so saying he hurried back inside the flower again.

The day wore on. The mayfly stayed where he was.

Another bee flew in clumsily. The mayfly screamed and the bee, too tired to argue, took off instantly. A ladybird tried to climb in and he screamed at her too.

'All right, all right. Keep your wings on,' she said huffily. 'Such manners. I wouldn't share your rotten old flower if it was the last one in bloom. But it's not, so there. I know some much better ones over the other side, the fashionable side.' And with a snort off she went and he was alone.

Some time later he took another peek outside. Just at that moment a couple of mayflies – newly-weds, he presumed – came by looking very pleased with themselves. 'Hello! What are you doing?' asked one of them.

'Living,' he replied.

'Oh,' they both said at once. 'Well, isn't it fun!'

'No, it isn't!' snapped the mayfly. He was beginning to get very tired of everyone telling him what fun it all was. 'It's hideous and frightening, and if you're looking for somewhere to hide you can look again. This is my flower.'

'Hide? Whyever should we want to hide?'

'Haven't you seen what's happening out there?' asked the cautious mayfly.

'Oh yes,' giggled the one.

The other, who was rather more serious-minded, said, 'Of course we have. But have you?'

'I've seen quite enough, thank you very much! And that's why I'm staying in here.'

'But think of what you're missing,' said the serious one. 'If you don't experience any of this wonderful day what will you have to look back on in your old age?'

'At least I shall have an old age,' he replied smugly. 'For obviously I shall live longer.'

'Oooh, do you think he could be right?' said the giggler.

'Nonsense. Don't listen to him. He's just a scaremonger, a coward!' And without wasting any more of their precious time off they flew.

'Coward? What's this coward?' the cautious mayfly cried angrily. 'Oh, what fools they all are, blind ignorant fools! But I know better, I've got more sense than any of them.' And to prove it he dived back inside.

The weather began to change. In the afternoon, heavy black clouds scudded across the sky, huge billowing shapes that drew nearer and nearer. Outside all grew quiet and still, and in the darkest, coolest part of the flower it was stifling, as though all the air had been sucked out and left only an empty space which would finally suffocate him.

'What new torture is this?' he moaned, but would not move to find out. 'Oh no, I'm not budging. No heroics for me.'

And then the lightning flashed and the thunder roared and the rain fell in thick drops that nearly flattened the beautiful flower, bouncing it up and down till the mayfly felt quite sick and giddy.

'Oh, this is surely worse than being snatched

by a fish!' And yet for all his fright he felt a sort of satisfaction, triumph almost. 'There, there!' he screamed as a fresh crack of thunder exploded overhead. 'Proves my point exactly. What chance would I have out there? Let them snigger and sneer, let them laugh, but we'll soon see who laughs longest. Why, after this I could be the only one left alive. That will serve them right!' And all through the storm he shivered and shook and praised himself for being so wise.

And then as suddenly as it all began, so it ceased. Out came the sun once more, and the air was filled with a cool sweetness. It was too tempting, even for a cautious mayfly. He crept to the front of the flower, just close enough to the edge for a good look.

An extraordinary sight greeted his eyes. He'd been expecting nothing but desolation and yet all around him was teeming with life – ants, worms, bees and birds, even mayflies. Hundreds of them. And the noise! He'd never heard anything like it: buzzing and croaking, twittering, gurgling and chirping. And through this dreadful cacophony came snatches of chatter – some of which, the mayfly realised, were about him.

Two beetles scurried by, deep in conversation: '... obviously not right in the head. Just sits in a flower and won't come out.'

'Silly fool,' replied his companion. 'Life is too short to be so careful.'

'Even shorter if you're not,' thought the mayfly. For a moment he considered setting forth to explain his motives to these imbeciles, but already they had passed out of earshot.

'He's a disgrace, making us a laughing stock,' said an angry mayfly voice quite close.

'Let's flush him out, teach him a lesson,' said another.

'Why bother?' said a third. 'He'll learn soon enough.'

'Learn? Learn what?' cried the mayfly indignantly, though of course not too loudly. 'How dare they be so high and mighty, the hypocrites! They must have sheltered too, else how could they survive?' It was all very puzzling.

Yellow evening sunlight rippled the surface of the pond. The mayfly, still puzzled, watched and felt strangely touched. It looked so peaceful, safe even. But then he thought of the worm, the fish, the other flies, and all the horrible dangers.

'No, no, be sensible,' he told himself. 'There's always tomorrow. It's been an eventful day and I survived. But now I'm really rather tired. This life is certainly exhausting. Perhaps after a good night's rest I'll get out and look around, perhaps do something, perhaps meet someone....'

But it was too late even for perhaps. No one had told him of a mayfly's lot. For all his caution and common sense his brief span was spent, and in the last blink of summer twilight he died.

An Unwelcome Visitor

Rat-a-tat-tat! Thus, for some, comes Death knocking at the door, expecting to make a grand entrance that cannot be ignored. She heard it all too well, and knew immediately. She was ready, but she could not move. Outside, the falling snow muffled the night sounds. An eerie glow pressed against the thin faded curtains. The room was cold and cheerless.

Rat-a-tat-tat came the knocking once more. She lay stiff, her eyes fixed immobile on a mottled brown patch on the ceiling where water from the flat above had once dripped through. Her throat in a tangled knot loosened just a little; her lips parted in a cry. But the cry was empty. No words came out. Unanswered the door opened anyway.

The little dog by her side on the bed had no need for words. He had lived his long life without speech; he could do without it now just as well.

The shadow, cold and sombre, advanced to the bed. The dog wagged his tail and growled: the one to signal that he was quite willing to be friendly and perhaps even to co-operate, the other to signal that he would nevertheless stand no nonsense.

The message was clear. The shadow moved no closer. 'Do not be afraid,' he said soundlessly. 'It is not for you I come, but for her.'

'We're ready,' said the dog.

'Not we,' said the shadow. 'Just her.'

'You can't separate us,' the dog replied, his fur bristling. 'We're together now and that's how we'll stay, wherever you must lead us.'

'Clearly you do not understand.'

'Course I do. I'm not stupid.'

'But you do not belong.'

'Not belong?' snapped the dog. 'Haven't I given her the best years of my life, looked after her, guarded her? Haven't I been her friend and constant companion? Who could belong more than that?'

The shadow sighed wearily. He was not prepared for explanations. He had a solemn duty to perform, and if only this wretched, impertinent dog–

'Her time is up,' he explained calmly. 'Her allotted span–'

'What about mine?'

'That will come.'

'Oh yes? And what happens meantime? Shoved in a home with a lot of strays – or worse. No, thank you very much.'

'Someone will take care of you.'

'Fat lot you know,' said the dog, warming to the

fight. 'Without so much as a "by your leave" you waft in here in the middle of the night and tell me to give her up just like that. You've got a nerve.'

'You are being very selfish.'

'That's as may be, but what do you expect?'

'I have my responsibilities,' said the shadow, beginning to lose patience. It had been a difficult night already. He was in no mood for argument. 'Try to see this from my point of view—'

'And will you do likewise for me?'

'In all things,' the shadow continued, 'there is a right time for coming, and a right time for going.'

'Obviously,' agreed the dog. 'And I've told you we're ready.'

'That is not possible. There are rules.'

'Hang your rules,' he growled.

Man's best friend, or so they say. As far as the shadow was concerned dogs were a confounded nuisance, being protective, poking their noses where they weren't wanted, not to mention other rather unpleasant habits. And why, he asked himself, are the little ones always the most belligerent? He had encountered similar problems all too recently – once with a Scottie, and once with a particularly obnoxious Pekinese. The humiliation made him shudder.

'I'm sorry,' he said at last, 'but this is the way it is.'

'You can't force her to go,' the dog answered gruffly.

The shadow stretched out an arm. He could not

reach. The little dog was right. The shadow had no real power there. He could coax, he could persuade, he could promise – but he could not force. Naturally there was no escaping in the end, but it was tiresome to have to come back a second time, or even a third, for what was so inevitable.

'Why don't you let her decide?' he suggested.

'Oh no! Do you take me for a fool? I know your sly ways. The poor old dear is confused enough as it is. Once you start filling her head with your soft words she won't know whether it's Christmas or Timbuctoo.'

This puzzled the shadow. 'I don't understand.'

'She won't know if she's coming or going,' the dog explained, then added, 'You're not very bright, are you?'

'Oh,' said the shadow, rather taken aback. He was not used to this sort of conversation, and certainly not with a dog. He struggled for a moment to say something clever, but when nothing came to mind he answered simply, 'I have my orders, and there's not much time.'

'Time is relative,' the dog replied smugly. That was something he'd heard before. He wasn't at all sure what it meant but he felt instinctively it was a smart and proper response. 'Talking of which, I've been with her fourteen years. Ever since she lost her mate. That counts for something.'

'It is not my place to judge.'

'High time it was then. Me and her, we're a pair.

People stop us in the street and ask–'

'Your circumstances are not my concern. Just results.'

'Well, this is one you're not getting. I'll tell you that for nothing! Look, let me explain–'

The shadow knew what was coming. He'd heard it all before. It had been so easy in the old days. He would go to collect someone when their time was up, and that was that. So often now there was disagreement or wrangling. Some wanted to go sooner than their time, some wanted to go later – while some positively did not want to go at all. It showed a sad decline in the accepted order of things. Usually he found that polite reasoning worked – with people, that is. But it didn't work so well with domestic pets, and in particular not with dogs. With them there was no reasoning.

Just as dogs can hear a higher frequency than humans, so they have a certain communion with the other side. This is a power they share with cats (though of course the dogs would never admit to such a thing). Between the two of them his job became a trial and left him sometimes completely at a loss. The best thing was to get it over and done with as soon as possible.

'What you say can make no difference,' he began, but the dog had other ideas.

'He was just like me, her mate. Came from up north where – in case you hadn't heard – we don't suffer fools gladly. Anyway, that's why she chose me. To remind her. Call it silly and sentimental if you will. You're right. Still, there's no harm in it. Course she's old now; a bit past it perhaps. But she's kind and considerate, probably more than most, and when you get to my age you appreciate that sort of thing. She says what I like to hear, treats me the way I like to be treated. Well, almost. Maybe I can't chase a cat like before, maybe my bark is worse than my bite, but I'm still reliable enough for her needs. So I'm hanged if I'll let you or anyone else toss me aside like an empty tin can. Talking of which, don't think I've suffered that disgusting muck she calls dogfood all these years because I enjoy it. I don't, but times are hard. We have to be sensible. Don't get me wrong: we take our pleasures where we can find them. And we'll take a few more too if we stick together. Here or elsewhere makes no odds to either of us, but don't let's have any more of that "allotted span" nonsense. If her time is up, then mine is too. We won't be parted.'

The shadow had expected something a little more convincing. 'That is all?' he said. 'But there's nothing special in what you tell me.'

'Special? I never claimed there was. We can't all go gadding about having adventures and being exciting and heroic. Us? Ha, that'll be the day. More like simple and dull. Still, I'm not complaining, and neither is she. And we're not asking for any favours. If you're going to take us both, all well and good. We're ready. If not, clear off back to wherever you came from and let us in peace.'

'I cannot take you.'

'Well, there you are then. It's settled. Goodnight.' The dog curled his lip, but whether in defiance or downright dogged mockery the shadow could not tell. Nor would he stay to find out. He could feel the warmth of dawn approaching. His time was up; he was needed elsewhere.

'I shall return,' he said at the door.

'I don't doubt it. But my answer will be the same,' the dog replied sleepily. 'And shut that door behind you. There's one hell of a draught....'

She awoke much later than usual. To begin with she couldn't think where on earth she was, then the mottled brown patch on the ceiling came into focus. So often the sight of that first thing in the morning filled her with a dark heavy depression: another day to get through. This time it was different. She felt lively, almost a stranger to the dismal surroundings.

The little dog nuzzled her face, his cold wet nose tickling her ear. 'Come on,' he was saying. 'Time to get up. So many things to do and this is just the day to do them.' He gave her cheek an impatient lick.

Suddenly she felt like giggling. So, she did. 'Now, now, Samson. Stop that. I'm awake.'

The dog jumped off the bed. He went to the window, and taking the curtains between his teeth dragged them apart: first one side, then the other. This was a morning duty he had long considered his alone. Sometimes it was the only way to get her stirring. Sunshine, made even more brilliant by the fresh crisp snow outside, flooded the room. By some magical process the winter rays streaming through the snowflake-crusted glass spread a rainbow on the threadbare carpet.

'Oh Samson, look at that!' she cried, clapping her hands in delight.

The dog scrabbled back onto the bed and licked her cheek again.

'You are a silly,' she said, folding her arms around him. 'Goodness, I've had such a dream, but not really a dream at all. We had a visitor last night, right here in this room. Yes, we did, so it's no good you looking at me like that. You were fast asleep, lost to the world with one of your doggy dreams, I expect. He was so…' she began, but the memory was fading fast even as she tried to catch it.

The little dog wriggled from her arms, jumped down and ran to the door. 'Come on,' he insisted. 'This is no time for dreams. Urgent calls to make.'

'He was strange,' she continued. 'All cold and serious. Wanted to take me on a nice journey, he said. Just me and him, all alone. Certainly not, I told him straight. I can't leave my Samson—'

The dog, scratching at the closed door, turned and gave a quiet woof of approval.

'Oh, get away with you!' she said, and giggled again. 'You wouldn't understand.'

'If only you knew,' replied the little dog. 'If only you knew.'

About...

Macmillan Cancer Support

In 1911, following the death of his father from cancer, Douglas Macmillan used his inheritance to found the Society for the Prevention and Relief of Cancer. His aim was to provide advice and information to anyone suffering with cancer, homes for patients at low or no cost, and voluntary nurses to attend to patients in their own homes.

Over the years, the name of the charity has changed but the purpose has not. Today, working with every NHS trust in the UK, and relying solely on donations, Macmillan is a source of medical, financial, emotional and practical support for more than five million people from the point of diagnosis and all the way through their cancer journey. With the core goal that no one should face the experience alone, Macmillan offers assistance medically with nurses, GPs, and healthcare professionals; financially by providing grants and welfare and benefits advice; emotionally via The Macmillan Support Line, and practically with comprehensive information and help at home.

For more, go to www.macmillan.org.uk

The Silver Line

Following the success of the children's helpline Childline, which she founded in 1986, in 2013 Dame Esther Rantzen created The Silver Line to provide friendship, information and advice for older people who may be lonely and isolated or suffering abuse and neglect. Through its specially-trained team the charity provides the only national, free and confidential helpline which is open 24 hours 365 days of the year (other than the Samaritans).

Since it was launched the Helpline has received over 1.5 million calls. Currently it averages some 10,000 a week, of which more than two-thirds come in during the night and at weekends when other services are shut, and people are at their loneliest and most vulnerable. More than half the callers say they have no one else to speak to. The charity receives no statutory funding and relies entirely on donations.

For more, go to www.thesilverline.org.uk

John Foley

John Foley is an actor, puzzle setter and audiobook producer. After years of stage work he turned mainly to writing and audio. He has scripted and voiced more than 600 programmes for BBC English/World Service. Other audio work includes adapting numerous plays by writers such as Alan Bennett, Brecht, Ronald Harwood, Ibsen, John Osborne, J B Priestley and Victoria Wood for World Service Drama and Radio 4, and producing audiobooks for Naxos and Random House of unabridged works by Boccaccio, Byron, Wilkie Collins, Dostoevsky, Thomas Hardy, Henry James, Kipling, Salman Rushdie, Anthony Trollope, Sir Walter Scott, Bram Stoker, H. G. Wells, Virginia Woolf and many others. Published work includes several 'recreational reference' books, a volume of musical anecdotes, stories for Disney comics and a number of graded readers for children.

'Seven Simple and Slightly Silly Stories' is the first of several collections of 'fables', which he began writing some years ago while staying regularly in Hans Andersen's house in Copenhagen.

Grant Cathro

Grant Cathro is an actor, screenwriter and illustration artist. He began his career in his early teens with comedy strip-cartoons for two major Scottish newspapers. The most successful of these, 'The Whirlies' and 'The Kids', ran weekly for many years. A prolific writer for teenage and children's television and with more than 500 produced scripts to his credit, he has been nominated for (and won) BAFTA, Royal Television Society, Writers' Guild of Great Britain and Prix Jeunesse awards. As an artist, Grant illustrated many episodes of BBC's 'Jackanory' and Thames Television's 'We'll Tell You a Story', and for Amber Lane Press has created covers for published plays by Anthony Shaffer, Ronald Harwood, Richard Harris, Bob Larby, Julian Mitchell, Peter Terson, Donald Freed, Maxim Gorky and Chekhov. Over the past decade, he has also provided comedy Christmas cards for the Actors' Benevolent Fund.

Grant is currently combining his writing and drawing skills to produce his first illustrated comedy novel.